Dragon Summer

A Magical Journey of a Boy and his Dragon Friend

THAATHWIK ARSHA ABHILASH

D1367672

pithal | pithal books

Dragon Summer

A Magical Journey of a Boy and his Dragon Friend

by

Thaathwik Arsha Abhilash

Language **English**

First Edition **December 2020**

Published by

 pithal books

Illustration **Animesh Xavier**

Book Design **Hisham**

ISBN 978-0-578-82865-7

*"We strengthen our community
and leave it better than we found it".*

KARATE AMERICA, WI, USA.

Dragon Summer

Foreword

Dragon Summer begins on an ordinary summer day, filled with sunshine, bike rides, and bird watching. But what starts out as an ordinary day, quickly turns extraordinary when Thaathwik meets Ash. Thaathwik realizes that Ash is unlike the other birds he has been watching. Ash, he discovers, is no ordinary bird.

I said, "Up Ash!". He flew up. I was thrilled! I was riding a dragon! He flew up to the clouds, and dived back down. The wind was flying in my hair.

Ash, his new dragon friend, takes Thaathwik on an exciting "Dragon Summer" adventure, filled with suspense, intrigue, and bravery. There are portals and kingdoms and shapeshifters. Along the way, Ash introduces Thaathwik to Peregroenix. Then, another dragon named Breeze joins them on their quest. For fantasy lovers, with this adventure, you are in for a delightful treat.

This book, written by Thaathwik himself, is a fantastical tale that reflects the creative thinker that he is. I first met Thaathwik Arsha Abhilash as a student in my second grade class. From the start, I noticed his bright smile and his inquisitive eyes. Thaathwik enjoys learning about new things, and he is passionate about his old favorites, such as the Peregrine Falcon. A preferred pick from second grade, Thaathwik found a way to weave this majestic bird into his story. Thaathwik sprinkles his innate humor throughout the book, helping us get to know the characters in the story better. He also includes pronunciations, facts, and descriptions which reflect Thaathwik's attention to detail. Writing was an important part of our second grade day, and I fondly remember right where Thaathwik sat, working enthusiastically on his books.

Now a fourth grader, Thaathwik is continuing to grow into an impressive writer. While learning at home, he set a goal to write a book, and he did just that. Through the pages of Dragon Summer we are treated to a spectacular journey filled with interesting characters who set goals, encounter obstacles, but continue to persevere. Embedded in these pages, we also find a hard-working writer, eager to share an imaginative story with the world. We find a young author using his imagination to weave a tale for others to enjoy. We discover how hard work, perseverance, and enthusiasm can help us reach our own goals.

Mrs. Indestad
Second Grade Teacher
Burleigh Elementary School

Preface

Just like most of the world, I also started the Corona lockdown days in March 2020. We were trying to be creative and engaged as much as possible, but it was not an easy task. The search for finding new ways of creative engagement put a spark in my mind to write a book and *Dragon Summer* is an aftermath of that thought.

This book is a story of a 9 year old boy and his dragon friend who set on an adventurous journey. The story will take you through different types of challenges the boy and his dragon friend have to face in their journey to accomplish a mission.

This is my first ever attempt in the world of fictional writing. I hope, you will have a good reading experience and I sincerely thank you for your support.

Acknowledgement

I'd like to thank My Mom, My Dad, my little brother Thadwith aka Dichu aka little 't', my families in the USA and back in India, friends of my mom and dad, Karate America Brookfield, Burleigh school teachers, Friends at Burleigh school, WISMA (Wisconsin Malayali Association) community, Animesh Uncle for the wonderful illustrations and Salish uncle for converting *Dragon Summer* to this beautiful book.

Chapter 1
Strange Bird

Schools were already closed, and it was the first day of summer vacation. My little brother and I were biking outside. It's been a couple of hours that we were outside. My dad came out and said, "It's been too long, it's time to go in".

"I'll stay out for a while", I replied.

"Ok", my dad answered. He took my brother inside the house. I put my bike in the garage and started watching the birds for a while. That's when in the sun, I saw an enormous bird! I couldn't see what type of A bird it was because it was right in front of the sun.

From a far distance, it looked like a tiny bird. But I could tell, it was a gigantic bird.

Chapter 2
Unexpected Creature

The odd, huge bird kept on flying up in the sky for some time. Then it swooped down and landed by our maple tree in the front yard. I realized that it was making no sound while flapping its wings. when it landed I gasped, I was so surprised! I've always wanted to see one in my life. Everyone said that this creature isn't real. But now I see a real one! No one will believe me until I show them. But, at least, my dream came true.

Chapter 3

Ash

The dragon sneaked up behind a squirrel. He was making no sound when walking. And then… Bam!!!. The squirrel was gone {in his tummy}. I slowly, hesitantly crept up to him. We met each other's eye for a second, then he leaped at me! I offered him some leaves. He breathed fire on the leaves, and they burned to the ground.

I went into the house and got some pieces of raw meat. I came back outside and the dragon was gone. I walked on to the driveway, I looked all around me. Then I heard a growl behind me. I looked behind and saw nothing. The Growl was there again, I looked at the roof and saw the dragon. I offered him one piece of the raw meat I took. He softly landed on the driveway, I slowly walked towards him and dangled it in front of his mouth. He watched it for a minute, then he ate it.

I gave him another piece, and then another, and another. when I gave him another one, he breathed fire on it. I was confused. I took a look at the piece of burnt meat. And I could see it!!! When he breathed fire, he wrote his name on the piece of raw meat. It said, 'ASH'.

Chapter 4

Magical Friend

I took a stick and wrote my name 'THAATHWIK' in the mud. Then I gave another piece of meat. After he ate that piece of meat, I closed my eyes, turned my head away from him, and touched his snout. Nothing happened to my hand. No fire on my hand, no bite marks, claw marks, or anything else that hurts. Then I realized he was putting his snout in my hand.

I gave him another piece of meat and got on his back. I said, "Up Ash!". He flew up, I was thrilled! I was riding a dragon! He flew up to the clouds, and dived back down. The wind was flying in my hair. And I saw that we were going right for the maple tree.

I didn't know what to do, I closed my eyes, waited, and waited. Then I felt a change of direction. I felt my head going back, and then my head went back straight again. He moved up all by himself! and he landed in the woods by my house.

Chapter 5
Home Sweet Home

I saw a big hole on the ground. I didn't know what it was. Then he walked over to a tree. I was like, "What are you doing!?".

"You'll see", He responded.

"You can talk!", I exclaimed.

"Very well, In fact, I can talk , write and read", Ash replied.

He gave me a smile, and I smiled back. Then he pulled a branch down like a leaver. Then the big hole split apart. And it showed a deeper hole, Except it was made of stone. In the middle of the stone hole, it said password.

"Al-Aziziyah", (Al-Aziziyah-tea), He said. The stone hole broke in half like the dirt hole.

"What language is that?", I asked.

"Arabic", he answered.

 "What does that word mean?", I asked.

"Well... It's a place"

"Why is that place the password?"

"It's the hottest place on earth", He answered. "Jump in".

"Huh?", He had already jumped in. So I jumped in too. "Are we falling?", I asked.

"Of course we are", he responded. That's when I saw a circle thingy that was blue and pink.

"We're going to hit it!", I exclaimed.

"Don't worry", He said. I was definitely worrying. How can I not worry? We were just about to hit it! I closed my eyes and turned my head away. Embrace for impact! I thought. 3...2...1... nothing happened. I opened one eye. All I saw was blue and pink dashes. I opened my other eye. Still, all I saw was pink and blue dashes. I looked to my right and saw Ash in the sea of blue and pink.

"Where are we?", I asked.

"In a portal", he answered. Then I understood why I felt nothing when we hit the portal. I looked straight forward and saw a ginormous cave with many smaller caves by the edges. I was going head first! And then we came out of the portal and landed in the huge cave. I flew out of the portal and hovered above the ground for a bit, and then I fell down. I looked around and I saw dragons all around. "This place was full of dragons!!! Amazing!", I thought to myself.

"Where are we?", I asked.

"Fire dragon's edge", he answered. "It's under the lut desert. The Lut desert is in Aziziyah".

"I thought it was Al-Aziziyah", (Al-Aziziyah-tea)", I said.

"Aziziyah is English".

"Hmm!", I exclaimed. "Where do we go now?".

"My place", he said. I didn't know where that was, so I just followed him to the cave straight in front of us. Once we entered I saw a dragon neighborhood. I saw dragons everywhere. Some of them looked at me with weird looks. Some of them looked surprised just like me. Then I heard my dad calling me.

"That's my dad, I better go", I said. "See you tomorrow!".

"Wait! Take this". He gave me a seashell. "Blow the tip if you want to call me. see you tomorrow!", he said.

"Thanks! Ok, see you tomorrow!".

Chapter 6

Peregroenix

I woke up the next day, remembering about Ash. I did not want to waste any time, so I quickly brushed my teeth, changed clothes, went downstairs and had breakfast. I couldn't wait any longer, I went outside. I took the seashell out of my pocket and blew the tip, waited for a minute by the dirt hole. There he is, I saw him, he came out of the trees on my right.

"Hi", he said.

"Hey!", I said. "Ready to go in?". I couldn't believe myself, that I asked about going in without any second thoughts, yes, I was so excited.

"Of course!", Ash said. I went over to the tree and pulled the branch Down. The dirt hole split apart revealing the stone hole.

"Al-Aziziyah", (Al-Aziziyah-tea), I said, no doubts - I had learnt the password yesterday itself. The stone hole split apart and showed us the stone passage. We jumped in, went through the portal, and came out on the other side to

fire dragon's edge. Once we got into fire dragon's edge, we walked into Ash's neighborhood. "What's your neighborhood called?"

"Dragon's corner", He responded. "You know what?".

"What?", I responded.

"I want you to meet someone", he said.

"Who?", I asked.

"The king", He responded.

"The king!?", I exclaimed.

"Yep!", he said.

"But... I'm not a dragon, I am not one of yours!", I said as I was a bit worried and tensed

"It's Okay. he welcomes all good creatures", he told me.

"Phew!", I exclaimed. "What's his name again?".

"Peregroenix", he said.

"Why does his name sound an awful lot like Peregrine Falcon?", I asked.

"Because he's a phoenix dragon", he said.

"what...?", I asked.

"When phoenix dragons are 3 years old, they get to choose another form, so they can patrol the Ground above", he explained. "they can turn into their alternate form whenever they want to. And then they can turn back".

"So... his alternate form is a peregrine falcon!?", I exclaimed.

"Yes, why do you sound so excited?".

"Because peregrine falcons are my favorite animals! They are the fastest on earth". I was so excited. I can't wait to meet the king, I thought.

"The king likes to stay as a peregrine falcon most of the time, and he has an evil twin brother named Peregroenix II", he explained. We entered the palace and saw the golden stairs gleaming in the chandelier's light.

"The king doesn't like anyone waiting so he doesn't give many appointments. And the king doesn't get many visitors in the summer".

We walked into the king's and queen's huge quarters. It was so big, enough for the king to fly around in.

There I saw four thrones. One for the king's peregrine falcon form, one for his phoenix dragon form, and two for the queen. The king was on his peregrine falcon Throne. The queen wasn't there. She must have been patrolling the ground above. The king saw us and transformed into his phoenix dragon form and moved on to his phoenix dragon throne. He was red and had a scar across one of his eyes. when he was in his phoenix dragon form he was bigger than me.

"It's alright! I love peregrine falcons! They're my favorite animals", I said.

"Oh! They're my favorite animals too!", he told me. He transformed back into the peregrine falcon form and moved back to his peregrine falcon throne.

"My name's Thaathwik", I said. Just then we heard a rumbling above. I didn't know what it was, but it sounded pretty dangerous. Ash and I went outside to see what was going on. Then I saw it. A black dragon, I saw he could just turn into a puff of smoke, so that he doesn't get hurt and hide. But he just turned back into solid when he was in the middle of transforming into smoke. I understood that he was a bad guy... but I didn't understand why he would turn back into solid. He left as fast as he entered. Now I was really confused. Maybe it was because he was scared of something. What could he be scared of here?, I was puzzled.

Chapter 7
Camo and his Alphas

I went to Ash and Peregroenix, I was tense.

"Who-was-that!?", I panted.

"Shadow!"It was Peregroenix who responded.

"Shadow broke us off the trail. We couldn't Deliver the message.", a wolf that came in said.

"Very well Camo. Where are your Alphas?", Peregroenix said.

"My alphas are right outside the door, Your Majesty", Camo (the wolf) said.

"Bring them in", Peregroenix said.

"Yes, Your Majesty. I will bring them right in", Camo said. He went outside the door and came back with his wolf pack.

"I have a mission for you Alphas", Peregroenix said. "Spy on Shadow".

"Yes, your majesty", said the alphas. Then all of them turned into Shadow's servants. Woah! I thought in my mind. They went off to Shadow's layer to spy.

"What were those things?", I said.

"Nature dragons", Ash said.

"Cool!!", I exclaimed. "Um... can you tell me more about Shadow?".

Chapter 8
Shadow

"Sure!", Peregroenix started saying, "Shadow is a shadow dragon. The shadow dragons used to be the swamp dragons allies. Till one day Shadow's great grandfather, Smoke, started a battle. There were burnt trees and dragon flesh all over the place". I had a freaked out look on my face, so Peregroenix decided to tell something funny, but also true. "There was also swamp goo all over the place". I had a kind of calm look on my face now. "The swamp dragons that survived realized that Smoke and all the other shadow dragons had put some planning into this. The shadow dragons went to their lair. Anyone can find that lair... but, no one enters, except the nature dragons. There are many layers of security. No one can slay a shadow dragon inside his/her lair, there's an enchanted spell that helps them survive in their lair. The owner of the lair has to give the spell to outside people so that they can survive forever in the lair". That was a pretty long description.

"So, can they die outside of the lair?", I asked.

"Yes", he answered. "Oh, and this reminds me... I have a mission for you too", After a pause, he said. "Trap Shadow".

"Are you talking to me, Your Majesty?", I asked.

"Yes, who else would I be talking to?".

"Uhhhh… Ash?", I said. "Why me!!! I can't trap Shadow. I have no armor! Or a sword. And plus, he's bigger than me!", I said.

"Then we'll be his size". I was confused. "With magic", He said.

"Wait, I need some time to decide", I said.

"You're gonna be a nature dragon. Take your time to dec-".

"I'll do it", I interrupted. Peregroenix laughed.

"There's one more thing you need to know. Shadow dragons are allergic to humans".

"So they sneeze if I'm near them?".

"No, their powers go away when you're near them".

"Now I know why he turned back into solid in the middle of transforming into smoke".

"This is gonna take half of the summer to do", he said.

"Wait, it's gonna take half of the summer to do the spell? Don't you just say some magical word like expelliarmus and turn me into a dragon?", I asked.

"Uhhh… no. We have to do some old school magic", he said.

"Do you mean, potions?", I asked.

"Yes", he said. Wait… how did you know?", he asked.

"I know a little magic", I said. "And… where do I get a notepad and a pen?".

"Over there", Ash pointed out.

"Thanks, Ash!", I said.

Chapter 9

Ingredients

I came back with a pen and notepad, "Alright, what are the ingredients?", I asked, I was in no mood to wait.

"The first ingredient is a fire dragon scale". I wrote that down and plucked a scale from Ash. and then I crossed that off.

"Check", I said.

"You are quick", Peregroenix chuckled.

"The second ingredient is a water dragon scale". I wrote that down too, I looked around. But I saw no water dragon.

"There's no water dragon here".

"The third ingredient is an earth dragon scale", he said. I wrote down earth dragon scale.

"The Fourth ingredient is an air dragon scale", he continued.

"Wait a second. If Ash breathes fire, and he's a fire dragon… then do you breathe phoenixes?", I asked.

"No, I don't breathe phoenixes, I am part of the fiirus

Draconis family. So I breathe fire too", he said.

"Let me guess, you're in the fire dragon family", I said.

"Yes, and a phoenix dragon's scientific name is, Fiirus fioneexa Draconis", (fee-rus-fee-one-eeks-a-draa-cone-iz), He said. I wrote down the air dragon scale. "Oh, you're gonna need 5 mint leaves for taste".

"Are we cooking now?", I joked. I wrote 5 mint leaves down.

"Alright, these are the last ingredients - A nature dragon's scale". I wrote that down. "And 3 devil fruits", he said. And I wrote that.

"What does the devil plant do?", I asked.

"If you eat the devil plant, you get horns", Peregroenix said. "We'll start our journey to aqua dragon city tomorrow", he said.

Chapter 10
Journey to Portal Dragon Bay

I woke up the next morning, I brushed my teeth , changed clothes and went downstairs to have breakfast. After I ate breakfast I went outside and blew the seashell. Today it was not only Ash, but Peregroenix also came.

"Hello, Your Majesty". I bowed. "Hey Ash", I said.

"Please, call me Peregroenix", Peregroenix said.

"Alright", I said. I had understood that Peregroenix is just first among equals or at least, he considered it that way, a real good leader.

"All aboard!!!", Ash said.

"Haha", I laughed. I got on Ash and peregreoinx just flew beside us. "Get on, we won't get separated that way", I told Peregroenix.

 "Alright", Peregroenix said.

"Hello and welcome to dragon airlines. I am your captain. And my name is Ash. We will be arriving at Portal dragon bay in 20 minutes", Ash had his own ways of making the

atmosphere light and funny.

"What?, I thought we were going to aqua dragon city!", I said.

"I know. But if we go to portal dragon bay then we won't have to wait 5 hours till we get to aqua dragon city".

"Are we going through a portal?", I asked.

"Yep!", Ash said.

"Yes!", I said happily. and We were off to Portal dragon bay.

Chapter 11

Portal Dragon Bay

"We're here!", Ash said. I sat up and looked down "uh… where is portal dragon bay?", I asked. All I saw was mud.

"Only (supposedly) fantasy creatures can see the bay, Unless a fantasy creature puts a spell on a non-fantasy creature", Ash said. "Like you". Ash put a spell on me so I could see the bay too. It was beautiful. There were dragons all over the place. Some were dining, some were on the stage, some were in the kitchen cooking.

"Could we dine there for a while?", I asked. "I feel hungry". All the smell and looks of the dishes had made my mouth watery.

"Fine, we dine for a while and then we go in the portal", Ash said.

"Alright", I said. We went down into the landing lot and landed. Then we went to the dining section and ate a while. The menu had lots of stuff. For the appetizer, I had chicken nuggets and alligator bites. For the main course, I had a bowl of mac 'n' cheese and some pasta. and for dessert, we just had some tasty brownies. and all of this for just 10 pieces of iron. For portal dragons, iron is money.

After food, Peregroenix took us to a nice portal dragon named Galaxy. Galaxy gave me some seaweed, I had to take it in so I could breathe underwater. It tasted awful! Peregroenix turned into his phoenix dragon form and peregroenix was way bigger than Ash in his phoenix dragon form. Ash, Peregroenix, Galaxy and I Went through the portal and landed right in the ocean. Then Galaxy went back to the bay. Then Peregroenix and Ash opened up their gills. "You have gills?!", I exclaimed. "I never knew that!", I said.

"All dragons have gills", Ash said.

"Cool!", I said. "Uh… where's aqua dragon city?", I asked.

"It's deep down there", Ash said.

"How long will this seaweed last for?", I asked.

"One hour", Ash said.

"I have to stay underwater for one hour?!", I exclaimed.

"The magic wears off in one hour, or after you go on land", Peregroenix said. We kept on diving down. And after half an hour, we found some more seaweed, just in case, it became one hour. we saw aqua dragon city after ten minutes. Ash said, "I think you should eat that seaweed now". I ate the seaweed and now I had another hour underwater (unless I came back to land). Now, all we had to do here is to get the aqua dragon scale.

Chapter 12

Aqua Dragon City

"Where is aqua dragon city? All I see is... is... what is it?", I said. All I saw was a bunch of pillars that fell down.

"You're not looking at aqua dragon city, You're looking at Atlantis". Ash turned my head and I saw aqua dragon city. I knew about Atlantis, from the history classes. Aqua dragon city looked kind of like Atlantis except the pillars were standing up. We walked up to the two tall pillars and Ash said "Atlantis". The water made a big ripple, and then we walked in. Once we walked in it wasn't seaweed and murky pillars anymore. It was a valley with so many blue dragons. The water was clear and transparent. It was so beautiful.

Chapter 13
The Whelps

"**W**oah!", I said.

"This is so cool!!!", Ash said.

"Wait, you've never been here Ash", I asked.

"Nope, Peregroenix just tells me all about it", Ash said.

"Guess that makes two of us", I said. Just then some baby water dragons ran over to us and knocked me over. then they started licking me.

"Guess you need to add some water dragon saliva to the ingredients list", Ash joked.

"Good one, Ash:-) Hey, Peregroenix. Can I stay with the babies for a while?", I asked. I always liked babies, now I know I like babies even if they are dragon babies.

"Yeah sure", I'll just make sure nothing's going wrong. Ash, can you stay with the baby's and Thaathwik?", Peregroenix said.

"Yeah", Ash said. I and Ash played with the babies for a while.

We played hide and seek, and tag. The Whelps never found me. After a few minutes, we went back to the valley and waited for Peregroenix. Peregroenix came a few minutes later.

"Everything's all right", Peregroenix said. "Come on guys, let's get that scale".

"I have to go whelps. I'll see you guys another time", I told the whelps. The whelps were sad. But at least I got to come back. Ash, Peregroenix and I went to get the water dragon scale. "Wait a second... can't we just get the water dragon scale from one of those whelps?", I asked.

"We need the scale from the king", Peregroenix said.

Chapter 14
Mini Lesson

I just was told, we need the scale from the king, I was not sure what that is so. "Why?", I asked.

"The king is the oldest water dragon. We need the scale from the oldest water dragon in the city", Peregroenix said and I nodded.

We got into the castle. and it had a ton of water fountains. The biggest water fountain was the one at the entrance.

"Woah… that fountain is as big as a Quetzocoatlus!", I said.

"Uhh… are you speaking english?", Ash asked.

"Yep, it's english", I said.

"Cool… can you tell me what a clappocloppus is?", Ash asked.

"It's called Quetzocoatlus", I said.

"Yeah… that thing. What is it?", Ash asked.

"The Quetzocoatlus was the biggest Prehistoric flying reptile. It was as tall as a giraffe when it was crawling. When it stood up it was bigger than a giraffe.", I said.

"So… basically a dinosaur?", Ash asked.

"No. There's a difference. Dinosaurs don't fly, and only a few of them gilded. Prehistoric flying reptiles on the other hand, flew", I said.

"Cool!", Ash said.

"You know a lot of stuff, now Is the school over?", Peregroenix asked.

"Yep", Ash and I answered together.

"That's good. Because we're here", Peregroenix said.

Chapter 15
The Water Dragon Scale

All I saw was a 20 foot waterfall.

"Is this a door?", I asked. "Because if it is, then it has no security. You can't even lock this door!", I said.

"There's a door behind it", Peregroenix said.

"Cool!", I said. Peregroenix did three stomps and breathed fire one time at the door. "What was that?", I asked.

"The password", Peregroenix said.

"Awesome!", I exclaimed. We walked in and the room had a ginormous dragon throne with a waterfall behind it! "This place is awesome!", I said.

"Hi, Aqua", Peregroenix said.

"Hi, Peregroenix. And you got company. who are they?", Aqua said.

"This is Ash; and this is Thaathwik", Peregroenix said.

"Hello, Your Majesty", Ash took a deep bow.

"Hello, Your Majesty", I took a bow like Ash.

"Hello to both of you too", Aqua said.

"We need something from you , Aqua", Peregroenix said.

"And what do you need?", aqua asked.

"We need one of your scales", Peregroenix said.

"One of my scales!? I have to go to a party tonight! I must look my best. How can I give you one of my scales!".

"We need the scale to make a potion", peregroenix said.

"You always have a good reason to make a potion. What's the reason this time?", aqua asked.

"We need the scale to trap Shadow", peregroenix said.

"Why didn't you tell me that before! I'd gladly give you the scale to trap Shadow!", Aqua said.

"Thank you Aqua", peregroenix said.

It felt like Aqua wanted to trap shadow as much as Peregroenix.

"Here, take this". Aqua took off one of his scales and gave it to Peregroenix.

"Here you go Thaathwik", Peregroenix said. The scale was as big as one of my hands!

"Uhh... do we have a bag?", I asked.

"We'll get one on the way", Peregroenix said. We went out of the city and into the water. There was some seaweed by the entrance so I took it and ate it. And then we came back to land.

"How do we get back to the bay?", I asked.

"We don't", Peregroenix said. Then he took some kind of rainbow stone and showed it to me and Ash. "This is a portal stone that galaxy gave to me. This will help us travel back home", Peregroenix said. He threw it up high in the air and breathed fire on it. Then the portal stone got bigger and bigger and became a portal. We jumped inside it and it led straight back home.

"Bye, see you tomorrow!", I said. "tomorrow where are we going again?", I asked.

"Earth dragon kingdom", Peregroenix said.

"Ok", I said.

Chapter 16

The Pentarge Day

Next day, I did my morning routine and went straight outside. I blew the seashell and Peregroenix came out on my right.

"Where's Ash?", I asked.

"Taking a morning stroll", Peregroenix siad.

"Does he usually do that?", I asked.

"Nope. he only does loopty loops when he's excited", Peregroenix said.

"I thought he was taking a morning stroll!", I said.

"I meant he was flying", Peregroenix said.

"Why's he so excited?", I asked.

"Because it's his pentarge day", Peregroenix told me.

"A pentarge what?", I asked.

"A pentarge day. It's a tradition for dragons", Peregroenix said.

"What do you do on a Pentarge day?", I asked.

"A pentarge day comes every 5 years. On your pentarge day you will grow bigger", Peregroenix explained.

"So… basically a birthday that comes every 5 years?", I asked.

"No, we have birthdays already. This is basically a day where a dragon grows larger. It happens every 5 years at 5:00 PM", Peregroenix said.

"So how do you know which day is your Pentarge day?", I asked.

"It's a scheduled date", Peregroenix said.

"I know it's a scheduled date but there must be a pattern like 6 months before your birthday or something", I said.

"Oh, the pattern is 4 months before your birthday", Peregroenix told me.

"So your birthday happens every year. But a Pentarge day comes every 5 years, 4 months before your birthday?", I asked.

"Yup!", Peregroenix said. Then Ash swooped down and landed on my left.

"Happy pentarge day Ash!", I said.

"Thanks Thaathwik", Ash said. "Just 9 more hours till I grow bigger".

"Uhh… how big will you grow again?", I asked.

"Around 16 Feet", Ash said.

"Ohh… just 16 feet. 16 feet!", I exclaimed. "I won't be able to fly you anymore if you're 16 feet!", I said.

"We'll find a way Thaathwik", Ash said. I calmed down after Ash said that.

"Ready to go to Earth dragon kingdom, Guys?", Peregroenix asked.

"Yup!"Ash and I said together.

Chapter 17

The Entrance

"Are we Going to fly?", I asked.

"No", Peregroenix said. "Stay here guys, I'll be right back", Peregroenix said.

"Ok", I said. Peregroenix went inside the dirt hole and then in the stone hole and into fire dragons edge. When he came back he had a portal stone in his mouth. He tossed it up and breathed fire on it. The portal stone got bigger and bigger until it was a portal.

"We're traveling by portal? Okay!", I said. We jumped into the portal , and in no time, we started our travel. The portal Was green this time. When we landed, I had no idea where we were anymore. "Where are we again?", I asked.

"Moscow", Peregroenix said.

"Are we in one of USA's Moscows?", I asked.

"Nope. We're in Moscow, Russia", Peregroenix said.

"Moscow, Russia?!", I exclaimed. "You do have another portal stone. Don't you?", I said.

"I don't have another portal stone. But I bet Jade and Cole will have one", Peregroenix said.

"Who are they?", I asked.

"The queen and king of Earth dragon kingdom", Peregroenix said. Peregroenix walked over to a tree and tapped it two times. Then peregroenix said, "MoskvaZIGON". It must've been the password. And then The tree split in half

"Was that Russian?", I asked.

"Yes, MOSKVA is Russian for Moscow", Peregroenix said.

"Cool!", I exclaimed. Then we Jumped in. I thought we were gonna land on hard concrete, and I was right. At Least I took karate lessons so I landed on my feet. So did Ash. But Peregroenix turned into his peregrine falcon form and flew down. "Is that what you always do Peregroenix?", I asked.

"Yes", Peregroenix said.

"That would be fun", I mumbled.

Chapter 18
Booby Traps

"So, Where's the King's and Queen's quarters?", I asked.

"Right down the hall", Peregroenix said. I looked down the hall and saw an open door. That must have been the Queen's quarters.

"No security?", I asked.

"Oh... there's a ton of security. "Only dragons can get through the booby traps", Peregroenix said.

"Booby traps!?", I Exclaimed.

"Yep!", Peregroenix said. We started walking and I walked onto a tile. That tile triggered the arrows.

"Arrows!", I exclaimed.

"Duck!", Peregroenix said. I ducked till all the arrows passed. Then there was this motion triggered. When I triggered the booby trap, all those spikes popped up on the ground.

"How am I supposed to get across this?!", I asked.

"I don't know", Ash said. I saw some rocks by the side of the spikes. I climbed on the rocks and got to the other side.

"That was easy!", I said.

"Watch out for the next one", Peregroenix said.

"What is the next- whoa!!", I exclaimed. The floor started to rumble. Then it split in half. I was going inside a pit! I held on to the floor and pulled my legs up, it was a real struggle. Finally, I was able to roll onto the floor.

Chapter 19
The Last Trap

"**W**hew!", I said. We were at the door now. I was happy. "There we are, So now we just walk in!", I said. I walked to the door, And... Bam!!! "What is this thing?", I asked.

"I think you know what that is", Peregroenix said.

"Is it glass?", I asked.

"Yep", Peregroenix said. Then I stepped on a tile and I heard a rumbling.

"What's that sound?", I asked.

"The last trap", Peregroenix said. "You should run", Peregroenix warned me. Then a big ball with spikes that could squish me came out of a hole in the top. Then the ball started to roll towards me.

"a spiked ball!? That's not good!", I exclaimed. I started running as fast as I can. Then I came to the pit. And the ball was right behind me! I jumped to the other side before the pit opened. Then the ball came to the pit. I thought the ball would get stuck in the pit. But the pit closed before the ball got to it! The ball kept on rolling.

Then I came to the spikes. And I climbed on the rocks to get to the other side, but the ball came to the spikes. The ball got stuck in the spikes. Then I carefully went on the rocks, trying not to touch the ball's spikes. Then after a few minutes, I got to the other side.

"That was one of the toughest things I ever did in my life".

Chapter 20
The Earth Dragon Scale

"Come on, let's go in", I said.

Then Peregroenix walked up to the door and said, "rock, stone, stone, rock, rock, stone, stone, rock". Then the door opened and we entered. The quarters were so big! But the whole thing was made out of stone. Even the thrones were made out of stone. The floor was very hard too!

"Hello Peregroenix!", Coal said. Coal was a dragon who was made of stone. And he had green hair. Probably because he's an earth dragon.

"Hi Coal!", Peregroenix said.

"Hi Peregroenix!", Jade said. She looked like Coal, except with shorter horns. "And who are they, Peregroenix?", Jade asked.

"This is Ash. and this is Thaathwik", Peregroenix said.

"Hello Ash. Hi Thaathwik. What brings you here today, Peregroenix? I know, you always have good reasons", Jade asked peregroenix.

"We need one of your scales to trap Shadow", Peregroenix said.

Shadow was really notorious, No questions were asked further, it was like Jade and Coal were very much on the same page with us already.

"Here you go", Jade said. she took off one of her scales and gave to Peregroenix. And Peregroenix gave the scale to me. The scale was around the size of my palm, and it felt like a rock.

"We need one more thing", Peregroenix said.

"What is the thing you need?", Jade asked.

"We need a portal stone to get back home", Peregroenix said.

"Here you go", Jade said. And she gave us the portal stone. Peregroenix threw the stone high up in the air and breathed fire on it. Then the portal stone got bigger and bigger till it was a portal. By now, I know how a portal works for sure. Then we jumped into the portal and got back home.

"See you tomorrow guys!", I said.

"See you later Thaathwik!", Ash and Peregroenix said.

"Tomorrow we'll be going to air dragon nation. Ok?", Peregroenix said.

"Ok!", I said.

Chapter 21
Air Dragon Nation

I woke up the next morning, I had a new routine now. I did my new morning routine, the new normal for me. I went outside, I was going to blow the seashell but Ash and Peregroenix were already there, so I didn't have to blow it.

"Hello Ash! Hi Peregroenix!", I said. "How are you!", I asked.

"I'm great!", Ash said. "Can you guess what's different about me?", Ash asked.

"Of course, You're much bigger than yesterday?", I asked.

"Yep!", Ash said.

"I'm also doing fine", Peregroenix said. "Are you ready to go to air dragon nation guys?", Peregroenix asked.

"Yep", Ash and I said together, we both had formed a very good bond by now. Peregroenix went into fire dragons edge to get a portal stone. He came back after a few minutes and threw the portal stone high up in the air, breathed fire on the portal stone. The portal stone got bigger and bigger till it was a portal. we all jumped into the portal. The portal was white this time. And within no time, we landed in air dragon nation.

Peregroenix stomped two times and the gates opened. The place was made with clouds. Everything was a cloud there. The buildings were clouds, the floor was clouds, even the rocks were made out of clouds! Suddenly I started sinking! Ash went under the clouds and helped me up. Then Peregroenix took some clouds and put it in my mouth.

"Swallow it", Peregroenix said. Then I swallowed the clouds and Ash let go of me. I thought I was gonna fall straight down. But instead I stood on top of the clouds. It was magical.

"I can walk on clouds!" I could not hide my happiness, I was literally on cloud 9 .

"It wears off when we get off of the clouds", Peregroenix said.

"Cool", I said.

Chapter 22

The Air Dragon Scale

"Follow me I'll take you guys to the palace". Peregroenix said.

"The palace?", an air dragon stopped us and asked. She was so beautiful and looked majestic.

"Yes, the palace. And who might you be?", Peregroenix asked.

"The name's Breeze", she said.

"Hello Breeze, I am so glad that we get to meet the queen herself, we can move things faster now. I'm Peregroenix", Peregroenix said.

"Hey Peregroenix, I have heard a lot about you from my dad and mom. Welcome to our kingdom"

"Oh Yeah, your parents were very good friends of mine. I am really Sorry that I could not come on the day when you were made the queen"

"It's okay, I can totally understand you being busy taking care of your kingdom". She turned to us and asked Ash, "who are you?".

"I'm Ash", Ash said.

"And you?", Breeze asked me.

"I'm Thaathwik", I said.

"Thaadwik?", she asked.

"No. Thaathwik", I said.

"Thaathwik?", Breeze asked.

"Yep", I answered.

"Don't worry, they are my own guys. We need something from you Breeze", Peregroenix said.

"What would be that?", Breeze asked.

"We need one of your scales", Peregroenix said.

"And Why would you need that? May I know please", Breeze asked.

"To trap Shadow", Peregroenix said.

"Ummmm... ok! Makes perfect sense, My scale can never have a better purpose", Breeze said. She took off one of her scales and gave it to Peregroenix. And Peregroenix gave it to me.

"Bye. see you later", Ash and I waved goodbye to Breeze.

"Bye", Peregroenix said. Then Peregroenix led us to the gates.

Chapter 23
Stranded

There's one problem guys", Peregroenix said after we got through the gates.

"What?", I asked.

"We don't have a portal stone", Peregroenix said.

"No portal stone!?", I was worried

"That's right", Peregroenix said.

"We're stranded in the middle of a desert!", I said.

"At Least we're close to Aziziyah!", Peregroenix said.

"How close?", I asked.

"1,559 kms away", Peregroenix said.

"Is that long?", I asked.

"Yes that's very long", Peregroenix said.

"Can you fly all that way?", I asked

"I don't think so", Peregroenix said.

I heard someone approaching us, "Someone's coming", I said.

"Hello!", someone said.

"Hey, Breeze?!!!", Peregroenix asked.

"I want to join you", Breeze said.

"Join us?", Peregroenix said.

"Yeah", Breeze answered.

"You are most welcome, queen.", Peregroenix said.

"I heard you talking, I need a portal stone", Breeze asked. And she took one, "Here", Breeze gave Peregroenix a portal stone. Peregroenix threw it up in the air and blew fire on it. Then the stone got bigger and bigger till it was a portal. We followed Breeze into the portal. And in no time, we landed in fire dragons edge.

"Tomorrow we'll be going to Australia", Peregroenix said.

"Ok!", Ash and Breeze and I said together. Ash took Breeze to the Flame Brothers' Inn, as Peregroenix suggested. I went back home, and Peregroenix went to the palace.

Chapter 24

Australia

I woke up the next morning and did my (new) morning routine. I went outside and saw Peregroenix, Ash and Breeze were already waiting for me.

"Are You ready?", Peregroenix asked. We all nodded. Peregroenix threw the portal stone up and breathed fire on it. Then the stone got bigger and bigger till it was a portal. Then we all jumped on it and we came out the other side.

"I forgot it would be night here", I said. Peregroenix and Ash yawned. "Why are you yawning?", I asked.

"It's night. we're kind of used to sleeping early", Peregroenix said.

"Oh, I usually sleep late", I said.

"I can say that, we were waiting for you there for almost 10 minutes", It was Ash who passed that comment. I was thinking about the hard times I gave my mom and dad by reading books even late at night, without going to bed.

"Let's find the devil plants", Peregroenix said. We followed

Peregroenix for a few minutes. Then we found the devil fruits. They were high up in the Devil tree.

"This is easy. We just walk into that tree and get the devil fruit", I said. Then I turned around and walked to the tree just then I heard some rumbling. I saw an Ogre coming out from behind the tree with a club!

"Who dares to enter my devil tree!", the Ogre was very angry.

"We just came here to get the devil fruit, for something good. But we can't reach it. Could you please help", I said.

"Run", Breeze whispered in my ear. I started stepping back slowly because I didn't want to startle the Ogre. Ash hid behind one of the bushes. Peregroenix just stood there and Breeze copied me.

"I'll help you. I love helping and I don't have any problem giving. It's just that I don't like anyone taking without asking. How many do you need", the Ogre said. Breeze and I stopped walking back.

"We only need three, and sorry, I thought no one was here to ask", I said.

"Alright!", the Ogre said. He walked over to the tree and picked out 3 ripe devil fruits and gave them to me.

"Woah!", I said. "It looks like a cactus rolled up in a ball!". I tried touching one of the spikes. But the spike just bent over! "It's mimicking a cactus!", I exclaimed.

"My name's Noah," The ogre said.

"It's nice to meet you Noah", I said. "We'll see you sometime later. We have to go now, we are in a hurry", I said.

"Bye! See you later! Thank you for stopping by", Noah said.

"We also need one portal stone", I said.

"I can give you that, Stay here", Noah said. He went inside the tree. And when he came out he had a portal stone in his hand. Then he gave it to us.

"Thanks", I said.

"No problem!", Noah said.

I was happy and was feeling proud of myself, I had started taking the lead, It was now like a mission I wanted to accomplish as much as Ash and Peregroenix wanted to. I was thanking my mom, who had told me that Ogres love to take respect and give respect.

Peregroenix through the portal stone high up in the air. Then he breathed fire on it. The stone got bigger and bigger till it was a portal. Then we jumped in and returned to Wisconsin.

"See you tomorrow guys", I said.

"I'm going to tell you where we're going only tomorrow", Peregroenix said.

"Ok. bye!", I said.

Chapter 25
Nature Dragon Kingdom

Next day morning, I was so excited and charged up to continue the mission. I had slept on time, so that I could get up early and not make my friends waiting. After breakfast, I went outside and blew the seashell. Ash, Peregroenix and Breeze came in no time.

"Where are we going?", I asked.

"You'll see", Peregroenix said. Peregroenix went inside and got two portal stones. Then he put one portal stone in my pocket and he threw the other one up. Then he breathed fire on it. And it got bigger and bigger till it was a portal. We all jumped into the portal and got to the other side. All I saw was vines. Peregroenix stamped the ground 4 times. Then the vines got untangled Revealing the other side. The other side was beautiful, there were trees and dragons everywhere!

"What is this place?", I asked.

"Nature Dragon Kingdom", Peregroenix said.

Chapter 26
The Last Ingredient

"Follow me", Peregroenix said. We followed Peregroenix to a big tree.

"Is this the palace", I asked.

"Yes", Peregroenix answered. We followed Peregroenix into the palace. After a few minutes we got to the queen's door. "Grey-wolf", Peregroenix said. Then the door opened wide and I saw… the outdoors?

"Isn't this the exit?", I asked.

"No, it is not", someone said.

"Who's there!?", I exclaimed.

"Down here!", someone said. I looked down and I saw two ants. One ant was a queen ant and the other was a male ant. I could say that as I had read a lot about ants.

"Talking ants!?", I exclaimed.

"I'm not a talking ant".

"Then what are you?", I asked.

"Does this give you a clue?". then she transformed into a red-tailed hawk.

"Transforming ants?", I asked.

"Nope", Peregroenix said. Then both of them turned into dragons bigger than Peregroenix.

"That's big", I said.

"Now do you know what we are?", she asked.

"Full grown nature dragons?", I asked.

"Yep", she said. "My name's Macro. It's short for macrocosm. I'm the queen. And this is Cosmo, the king", Macro told me and Ash.

"And this is Viento, and this is Kai", Cosmo said.

"Hello!", I said.

"Aww, they're so cute!", Breeze said

"Hi", viento said.

"Hello", Kai said.

"Hi again Viento and Kai, this is Ash, this is Thaathwik and this is Breeze", Peregroenix said.

"Hi!", they both said.

"We are so glad that you thought to visit us Peregroenix?", Macro asked, "You always have good reasons, what is it this time".

"We need one of your scales to trap Shadow", Peregroenix said.

"Okay", she said. With no hesitation, She took off one scale and gave it to Peregroenix. Then Peregroenix gave it to me.

"Thank you", Peregroenix said.

"See you later guys!", I said.

"Bye!", Ash, Peregroenoix, Breeze and I said together.

"Bye!", the royal family said. Peregroenix opened the door and we walked out.

"Take the portal stone out of your pocket", Peregroenix said. I took the portal stone out of my pocket. Then I threw it up in the air and Peregroenix breathed fire on it. Then it got bigger and bigger till it was a portal. we all Jumped in. After a few minutes, we all wrapped up the day and went to our own shelters.

Chapter 27
Waiting

Next day morning, I had to do one extra task - pick 5 mint leaves from our vegetable garden. My dad was not so sure why I need mint leaves, but he was okay for me to pick them as mint leaves are healthy and won't do any bad.

"Alright! I'm ready to drink it", I said.

"You have to wait a few days till you can drink it", Peregroenix said.

"What!", I exclaimed.

"It will take a few days to make", Peregroenix.

"I thought he was going to drink It now", Breeze said.

"Nope, we have to wait a few days", Peregroenix said.

"Alright", I said. I handed over all the ingredients to Peregroenix, he went to make the potion with Ash and Breeze and I went back home.

"That was a pretty short day", I told myself. I had started loving those long exciting days.

Chapter 28
The D-day

I kept on going back to fire dragons edge to see if the potion was done. On the 5th day, my dragon friends came with happy news, the potion was done.

"So, I can drink it now?", I asked.

"Yes", Peregroenix said. He gave me a part of the potion and I drank it. It tasted weird, even with mint leaves in it. Suddenly I started feeling some vibrations, then I started getting dizzy. I felt very tired, and I fainted. When I woke up, I saw Ash, Peregroenix and Breeze looking at me.

"Try thinking of an animal and close your eyes", Peregroenix said. I thought of a Peregrine falcon and I closed my eyes. When I opened my eyes, I could see way farther, just like a Peregrine falcon! I looked at my hands and I saw wings!

"Did it work?", I asked.

"Were you thinking of a bald eagle?", Peregroenix asked.

"No, I was thinking of a Peregrine falcon", I responded.

"Well… You're a bald eagle", Peregroenix said. I tried one

more time. This time my wings looked gray.

"Did it work now?", I asked.

"Yeah", Peregroenix said. I quickly transformed into a cheetah.

"Yaay! I can transform!", I exclaimed.

"It worked!", Peregroenix said. "Let's go!", Peregroenix said. Peregroenix went and got Camo and his army. Then Peregroenix threw the portal stone up. After a few minutes we reached the Shadow palace. I transformed into a nature dragon and waited.

Chapter 29

The Ambush

"Does he know we're coming?", I asked.

"No it's going to be an ambush", Peregroenix answered. "Here's the plan. Transform into a shadow dragon, Go inside and tell Shadow I'm outside. He'll want you to capture me. Next, take me to Shadow. Then the rest of the army will trap the other shadow dragons and I'll help you trap Shadow. Then we put them into a human prison so they get the presence of a human", Peregroenix said. I transformed into a shadow dragon with the army, then went inside to begin the ambush. I found the main entrance and started looking for Shadow's quarters. Then I saw a shadow dragon standing by the wall.

"Uh… excuse me where is Shadow's quarters again?", I asked.

"Go straight and you'll see some stairs, go up the stairs and take the door at the end of the hall", he said.

"Thank you", I said.

"Hmm…", he said. He was on to me. I ran as fast as my

dragon legs could carry me, I followed that shadow dragon's instructions and took the door at the end of the hall. I almost opened the door but I thought, I better knock. So I knocked on the door and I saw Shadow at the door.

"This better be good", he said.

"I got Peregroenix, he is outside... sir", I didn't know if I should say sir or not.

He gave me a suspicious look and said, "Great, Bring him in". I went outside and brought Peregroenix in. Once I got into Shadow's quarters, Shadow looked at both of us. "I was expecting you Peregroenix", I didn't see Shadow giving a wink to Peregroenix. But I did realize Shadow emphasized Peregroenix's name. I figured out something was going on but I didn't know what.

"Attack!", Peregoenix exclaimed. I turned into a human and stood there. I was hoping that I could make Shadow not turn into a shadow. But he just kept coming at me. I dodged him by turning into a shadow dragon. He tried to attack? I thought I was supposed to be attacking!

"Peregroenix, why isn't his allergies kicking in yet!? And why aren't you helping!?", I asked.

"I am helping", Pperegroenix said. Then Peregroenix tried attacking me!

"What are you doing?", I exclaimed.

"Don't you see!? I'm helping Shadow!", he said. Both of them started attacking me at the same time. I kept on dodging them.

Then I turned into a nature dragon and earth-bended the ground so there was a barrier between me, Shadow and Peregroenix.

"I thought you were on my side!", I told Peregroenix. Shadow got through the wall so I broke down the wall and started fighting again.

"Peregroenix is on your side. But I am on Shadow's side!", he said.

"Peregroenix II !!!?", I asked.

"You finally figured it out!", Peregroenix II said.

"Where's Peregroenix!?", I asked.

"I'll never tell you!", he said.

"Then tell me why Shadow isn't allergic anymore!".

"Because Camo duplicated the Ingredients for us! Then I made the potion and Shadow drank it! Now he's a nature dragon", he said.

"So, Camo's on your side too!?", I exclaimed.

"No! We tricked him into doing it!", Peregroenix II said.

I turned into a shadow dragon and went to the library as a shadow. I was hoping to find something in library books that could help me, mom always said, books are the best friends anyone can ever have. I went into the magic section and found a book called, All About Potions.

I found the chapter about reversing and I got to the nature dragon potion page. It said, if you drink the nature dragon potion one more time then you reverse the potion. You can drink it again after- -reversing the potion. If you drink it again you can become a nature dragon again. Or you could just not reverse it. I got the answer! I figured out that there should be a secret compartment where Shadow's hiding the potion. I quietly walked into the royal zone.

"Hey! Hey you!", a guard said. "Royalty only in this zone!", he said.

"Oh, the king sent me to get a book for him from the royal zone", I quickly made something up.

"He usually gets his books by himself", the guard said.

"He is very, very busy right now. That's why he sent me", I said.

"Hmmm... okay!", he let me inside. I found the place where Shadow keeps all his books. Just then a few of Aamo's alphas came and took the guard. I knew that when someone has a secret compartment they usually use a book as a lever. Then I found a book with the title, All about Shadow. Then I found another copy of the book. I tried taking the first one, nothing happened. I took the second book and the book shelf split open. I walked inside and transformed back into a human. I saw a cauldron with nature dragon potion, also, I saw a few small pots on a table. I walked over to the table , took a small pot. Then I took a bit of the potion in the pot, closed it and put the pot in my pocket. When I turned around, I saw a door. I opened the door and to my surprise, I saw Peregroenix and another dragon tied up, I've never met the 2ns dragon before. I quickly untied them.

"Hi Peregroenix", I said.

"How do you know my name!?", he asked.

"I came with Ash and Breeze", I said.

"Who's Breeze?", Peregroenix asked.

"I'll explain later", let's escape first, I said.

"Ok, just tell me what's going on", Peregroenix said. I quickly

summarized what was going on and then I transformed into a shadow dragon and walked out of the library. I took Peregroenix and the other dragon outside. In the shadow form itself, I went upstairs to Shadow's quarters and entered the room.

I saw Shadow talking to Peregroenix II. I quickly tried to attack Shadow but I missed. Then he tried to attack me. Peregroenix II came and helped Shadow. They kept on missing, I was able to slide away from their attacks.

"Aren't you going to say anything, Shadow!? Or are you just going to stay quiet and be a scaredy cat!?, I said mockingly.I wanted to provoke him.

He got annoyed and said something, "I'm going to ge-". I was waiting for this moment, in a split of milliseconds, I put some nature dragon potion in his mouth before he could finish his sentence. Then I turned into an anaconda and shut his mouth until he swallowed it. After he swallowed it, I turned back into a human and his allergies kicked in. Camo and his Wolf pack joined me by now, They had made sure that no guards were left to fight with us. I trapped Shadow and Peregroenix II in rock till we got to their prisons. We put Peregroenix II in a prison made of thick ice so he couldn't breathe fire. and we put Shadow in a human prison so he couldn't turn into a shadow again.

Chapter 30

Mission Complete

After everything was done, I met the other dragon who was in the room with Peregroenix.

"Hi, I don't think we met. I'm Squirroenix. I'm the queen of fire dragons edge. I got trapped by Peregroenix II with Peregroenix", she said.

"Oh, so that's why I didn't see you when I met Peregroenix II ! I'm Thaathwik", I said. Peregroenix came with a portal stone in his hand.

"Ready to go home?", Peregroenix asked.

"Yeah", I said. He threw the stone in the air and breathed fire on it. I returned home, my dragon friends went back to their kingdoms promising me that they would come and visit me once in a while. Thus the most exciting dragon summer came to an end, and in 1 month, the 4th grade starts. I have a lot of stuff to share with my friends, Ash had promised to show up in school once for my friends so that they will believe the "Dragon Summer" I had.

about
the author

Thaathwik Arsha Abhilash, 9 year old, lives in Brookfield, WI, USA with Mom, Dad and little brother Thadwith. Thaathwik is a 4th grade student in Burleigh Elementary School, Brookfield.

He is a Karate black belt and working towards higher degree black belts. Thaathwik is an Art enthusiast who loves movies, music & dance. Thaathwik finds happiness in reading, drawing, painting & playing with his little brother.

Dragon Summer is Thaathwik's 1st ever published book, Thank you all for the support and reading *Dragon Summer*.